The True Beauty In You

BY STEPHANIE–JOY GRIGG

Illustrated by LaTique Albergottie
Revised Design by Taneki Dacres
Edited by Krystal Berry

ISBN: 978-0-578-67002-7 (Paperback)

This is for You...

To the black women who inspire me...

To the Women in Ministry that pray for me...

To all of the little girls who motivate me...

To my sorority sisters who cheer for me...

To my family and friends that believed in me...

To a special friend who believed in my work for girls but was not able to see the completion of this book...RIP Meagan Robinson...

To ALL of you...THANK YOU.

Last but not least, a special thank you to Sheilah Vickers, Maranda Curtis and Krystal Berry for your guidance on this project.

"Good morning, my princess. It's time to rise and shine!"

YAWN... and with a good stretch Madison-Joy replied, "Good morning, Mommy!" Peeling the covers back, she immediately thought of seeing her friends again at school.

After taking a shower, she rolled her eyes anticipating her not-so-favorite part of the day: Getting her hair done.

$\mathcal{M}$argaret returned to the room, with smiles, to collect needed items to brush her daughter's hair. Madison-Joy sat unenthusiastically in her chair as she did each morning. "Mommy, can't we just leave my hair like it is and stick a bow on the side?"

"Oh, no! I wouldn't think of it. Every princess deserves to be beautiful every day," said Margaret.

Madison-Joy shouted, "But Moooooommy! I'm not a princess!"

'Why, of course you are" said her mother with a smile! And she began brushing her daughter's beautiful, thick and curly hair into a puff on each side while singing,

It's a beautiful day to be a princess.
Who knows what the day will hold?
It's a wonderful day for a princess,
To be beautiful, fearless, and bold!

All of a sudden, Madison-Joy felt the pain of the brush
and yelled out, "*OWW!*"
Her mother replied, "I'm sorry, sweetie. Did that hurt?"

"I don't know what it is," Madison-Joy said,
"But you always put that hard,
prickly thing on my head. My hair is thick enough.
I don't see why I need anything else
besides my huge puffs."

Mommy responded, "Ahh, that's your..."

And before mommy could finish, Madison-Joy
interrupted her and said,
"No, Mommy. It's not. I'm not a princess, okay?
I don't look like the other princess girls in my class.
I'm not pretty like them.
My clothes don't look like theirs either.
I don't have anything in common with them.

I wish I were a princess, but I'm just me — a regular black girl with bushy hair and this hard thing you stick on my head every day."

$\mathcal{M}$argaret sighed and hugged her daughter.
"Madison-Joy, I know you'll see what I see
one day soon," she said.
"Now, would you like to take a look in the mirror to check
your outfit and hair before you go to school?"
"No, ma'am," Madison-Joy replied.
She just shook her head and walked out of the
bedroom and headed towards the front door.

When Madison arrived at school, she went straight to Mrs. McCoy's room and soon saw her classmates. Before walking toward them, she observed the other girls in her class. They were laughing and chatting on the blacktop awaiting the bell to enter the building. How she longed to be regal and beautiful like them.

She thought to herself,

"Oh, look at Meaghan...now, talk about a princess!"

Her long, silky black hair was adorned with a sparkly light blue ribbon that flowed down her back with her hair.

And there's Porshia. She's a princess too.

She wore a glittery red and gold sash that crossed from her left shoulder to her right hip.

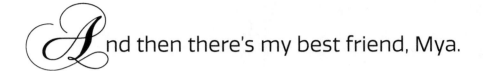

nd then there's my best friend, Mya.

Mya always listened and understood Madison-Joy most when she would tell her that she didn't feel like the other girls. But Mya would always say, "Joy-y, you're such a nice person. Don't worry about the other stuff."

Madison-Joy was proud of how nice she was: she always said "please" and "thank you," she made sure to say her grace before eating, she said her prayers each night before bed, she never teased or bullied the students in her class, and she even always said, "yes, ma'am/no, ma'am," or "yes, sir/no, sir" to adults. But she often thought to herself, "Why can't I be a beautiful princess like them? Even Mya carries a shiny scepter."

Madison-Joy looked down at herself and nothing about her said princess.

"Alright, class. Let's line up," called Mrs. McCoy. "We have a special day planned for you all."

Cheers erupted from the students walking into the building and into the classroom. As they emptied their bookbags and sat at their desks, they awaited the special plans that were arranged for them.

Mrs. McCoy continued, "Today, we will have a guest artist visit our class!" Excitement filled the air with applause and group conversations in the classroom.

"Our guest will teach us about using modeling clay and we will create sculptures here in class," she responded.

"Umm...Mrs. McCoy, are we going to make statues as big and tall as we are?", asked Ray. With a smile, she replied, "No, Ray. Mr. Edmund will explain further, but we will create a 3-D model of a person's head and shoulders."

Soon Mr. Edmund and his team entered the room and were introduced to the class. Sheets were spread across each desk and aprons were given to each student. After watching and working with Mr. Edmund, to get used to working with clay, the team worked with students who were divided into pairs. The assignment for each student was to create a sculpture of their partner.

*S*uddenly, hearing the assignment, Madison-Joy felt so sorry for her partner Meaghan.

"She's so beautiful and so much like a princess. And I'm so regular", thought Madison-Joy.

The project took several weeks to complete. The students added color and fancy ornaments. This made Madison-Joy feel even more self-conscious. She wondered how quickly Meaghan would finish her task of creating her statue.

She almost apologized for not being like all the other girls and not being enough to have something that looked pretty. Nevertheless, she busied herself with making a statue that looked most like the beautiful Meaghan. She did this to the very best of her ability and even included the sparkly light blue ribbon that adorned Meaghan's long hair.

The day arrived when each student presented their project and would give it to the subject. The sculptures were all covered with the artist's name on the canvas. Madison-Joy soon presented her model of Meaghan to the class and then to Meaghan. Meaghan was ecstatic about how life-like her sculpture looked!

"She's beautiful! Thank you, Madi!"

It seemed that it took forever for Meaghan's turn to come. And finally, when it was Meaghan's opportunity, Madison-Joy dreaded having her sculpture presented to her. She thought to herself, "Why is Meg so amped to give me this plain thing?"

ut Meaghan uncovered her sculpture and explained how she created it just as the other students did. Brilliance and colors of splendor were everywhere, but the brightest reflections of light came from the head of the sculpture.

"Meaghan," exclaimed Madison-Joy! "You didn't have to make fun of me and make up stuff," she cried. "What do you mean? It looks just like you, Madi," exclaimed Mya! "Well, what are those gold and bright colors on the head" asked Madison-Joy?

Madison-Joy couldn't believe her eyes! She looked at herself and then at the clay model. She looked at herself again and tears began falling down her face. What she thought was wild bushy hair was folds of curls. And what she thought was this hard, prickly item on her head was the most brilliant tiara she'd ever seen. It even had stones that glistened with each turn catching the light.

All the way home, Madison-Joy looked at Meaghan's creation with such pride!

She burst through her front door to greet her mother and recounted her day. With so much excitement, she said, "Mommy, it's me! It's me! I never knew that I'm a princess."

$\mathcal{M}$adison-Joy looked up and asked, "Mommy, am I really this beautiful?"

"Absolutely, princess! I don't think you've ever really looked at yourself long enough to notice," her mother said.

Madison-Joy thought for a moment and then asked, "So, Mommy, am I really a princess?"

Margaret replied, "You certainly are. Like every little girl, you just have to realize the *true beauty in you!*"

THE END

About the Author

Stephanie-Joy Grigg, a native of Queens, New York, is passionate about encouraging and cultivating the character of the next generation of young ladies. In 2009, after completing high school in three years, Stephanie-Joy earned a Bachelor of Arts in Psychology from Hampton University in Hampton, Virginia. She then continued her studies abroad at the Royal Holloway, University of London in England

Stephanie-Joy, after returning to the states almost a year later in the spring of 2013, completed the Master of Science in Education with a concentration in School Counseling from St. John's University in Queens, New York. In May 2018, she graduated with the Master of Divinity Degree from Princeton Theological Seminary, and she is currently pursing her Doctor of Ministry from the Samuel DeWitt Proctor School of Theology at Virginia Union University in Richmond Virginia.

Stephanie-Joy also serves as the Chaplain of the Hampton University National Alumni Association and is likewise a proud member of Alpha Kappa Alpha Sorority, Incorporated.

CPSIA information can be obtained
at www.ICGtesting.com
Printed in the USA
BVHW022227020520
579089BV00005B/483